JEFFREY'S JUNGLE

Written by Reid Genauer
Illustrated by Alan Close

Jeffrey's mother had to leave him home
to go out to the store.
If he got scared while she was gone,
he was to go next door.
She left him lunch, gum to chew and
the number she was at.
He was not to tease Jake the dog
or to touch the thermostat.

At first Jeffrey was content
to do as his mother wished.
After looking at the thermostat
Jeff could not resist.
To start he pressed it gently
and the heat was warm and good.
When Jeffrey finished pressing,
it was 90 where he stood.

Nothing seemed to change,
though it was hotter, that was true.
But turning up the thermostat
did not seem wrong to do.
That was just before he noticed and
he had an awful feeling the
potted plants that once were small
were growing from the ceiling.

Vines were wrapped around the couch
and strangling the chair.
A fish swam down a waterfall,
that was flowing down the stairs.

The kitchen was a swamp-land
where fifteen hippos fed.
They gobbled up the microwave
and ate the doggie bed.

There were lizards in the bedroom,
and a shark was in the tub.
Jake the dog was running
from a grizzly and her cub.

Jeffrey sat there staring,
he was sucking on his thumb.
A monkey sat there with him,
blowing bubbles with Jeff's gum.

In the midst of all this nature,
through a herd of zebras grazing,
Jeffrey heard the rattle
of his mom's garage door raising.

Well this simply wouldn't do,
Jeffrey quickly realized that.
So he raced straight through the grassland
to turn down the thermostat.

The temperature came crashing down
and with it came the vines.
The animals that still remained
went marching out in lines.

The swamp-land up and vanished,
disappeared before his eyes.
The water had all dried up,
The plants were back to size.

Mom would never see the swampland
or the mess it seemed to make.
But the doggie bed was missing,
"Jeff have you been teasing Jake?"

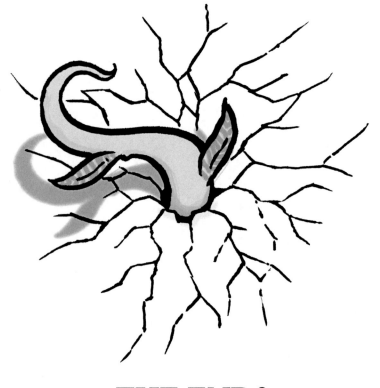

THE END?

Reid Reinhold Genauer is a singer, songwriter, storyteller and entrepreneur. He lives with his wife Rebecca and their three sons Ryder, Cole and Jed in Menlo Park, California. While they have never turned up the heat to 90° they do welcomingly embrace mischief in virtually every other form.

Alan Close draws. A lot. Cars, bunnies, flames, bikes, zombies - you name it. He lives with his wife Sara and their two sons Lucas, and Neven in Grand Rapids, Michigan. Don't ask how he and Reid became friends because it's an old, long and convoluted story that neither of them probably remember very accurately.

29816399R00015